The Swamp King's Daughter

Hans Christian Andersen

Illustrated by Tiziana G...
Translated from the ori... n text
by Marlee Alex

Scandinavia

Storks are fond of telling their children tales about things which happen around swamps and marshes. The first stork couple who told this tale had witnessed it themselves. They had their summer residence on a Viking log house, close to a fjord in northern Denmark. One evening the father stork returned home later than usual. His feathers were ruffled. He looked very upset!

"I have terrible news!" he exclaimed.

The mother stork was sitting on her eggs. "Don't tell me!" she replied. "You know it will distress me, and that will go right into the eggs!"

"You must know!" the father stork answered. "The princess, the daughter of our Egyptian landlord, has been here. She actually had the courage to make the trip, and now she has disappeared! She came disguised in a feathered cape together with the two other princesses. I saw them through the reeds at the swamp tonight. The three of them flew down and landed on the trunk of a fallen alder tree, flapped their wings and looked around. Then one of them cast

4

off her cape (it was the princess) and asked the two others to hold it while she dived into the water to pick a flower. But instead, they flew into the air with it.

" 'Dive!' they called to her. 'Never again will you fly in a swan disguise. Never again will you see Egypt!'

"The princess moaned and cried. Her tears ran down onto the alder tree. It began to move. What looked like a tree trunk was the swamp king himself! He turned over and lifted his long, mossy arms. As the princess jumped away, she sank into the muddy swamp. The tree trunk went down at the same time. Big, black bubbles rose to the surface of the water, but left no trace of what had happened."

"Oh dear," answered the mother stork. "You should never have told me about it. It will spoil the eggs! The princess can take care of herself I am sure."

5

A long time passed. Then, very early one morning, the father stork noticed that a green stem had shot up through the water of the swamp from the depths below. There was a leaf growing on the stem and a bud at the very top. The bud gradually blossomed in the warm rays of the sun. Right in the middle lay a pretty baby girl who resembled the princess from Egypt. The father stork came to the conclusion it must be her child by the swamp king.

"I cannot just leave her there," thought the stork. "But my nest is too crowded as it is. I know what I'll do! I'll take her to the Viking chief's wife who has no child of her own, though she has desperately wished for one. Since they credit me for bringing babies, I might as well do it for once."

So the stork flew back to the log house with

6

the child and laid her at the breast of the Viking woman. When the woman awoke, she was overjoyed. She kissed and cuddled the baby. But the tiny girl kicked and squirmed, crying hysterically. Finally, the child cried herself to sleep and lay sweetly on the bed.

The happy Viking woman began to dust and to scrub, and to prepare her house for the return of her husband and his men. She figured they might arrive just as unexpectedly as the child had done! By early evening she was exhausted. She lay down and fell sound asleep.

7

Shortly before sunrise the next morning the woman woke up and felt for the baby. It was not there! The woman grabbed a piece of live kindling from the fire and looked around. There, at the foot of her bed, sat a large, ugly frog. It looked up at her with strange, sorrowful eyes and gave a faint, helpless croak.

Just at that moment, the sun cast its rays through the cracks in the door and onto the bed. As it did so, the wide mouth of the frog

8

shrivelled into two small, pink lips. Its limbs changed into smooth, white arms and legs. On the bed lay the beautiful baby girl again.

"This must be a wicked dream!" said the Viking woman, as she clutched the baby to her heart. But the little girl tore at her and thrashed about like a wild kitten.

Another day and night passed before the Viking woman realized that the child was bewitched. By day she was as beautiful as a fairy, like her mother, but had an angry disposition. By night she took on the appearance of a slimy swamp creature like her father, but had a quiet, whimpering nature and sad eyes.

The Viking woman worried and wept over the child. How she pitied the poor thing! She dared not tell her husband the truth, but determined that he would only see the child by day.

One morning there was a rush of stork wings upon the roof of the log house. Hundreds of storks were gathering there for their annual flight south. As they flew away, a large bell began to clang. The Vikings had returned with rich plunder from far off coasts! Once again there would be feasting and festivity in the Viking residence by the swamp.

The Viking chief was pleased with the beautiful child who was new in his home. He liked her wild temper best of all. He boasted that she would be able to fight the most gruesome battles and to meet the worst kind of danger without blinking an eye. He never found out how her soul and body changed each day at sundown. His wife, however, grew to care more for the poor frog with its deep sighs than for the little beauty who bit and tore at everyone around her.

The raw, damp autumn fog crept over the marsh. The sparrows took over the storks' nest. But where had the storks gone? They were now in Egypt, where the winter sun is as bright and warm as it is on an especially nice, summer days in Denmark.

12

The stork couples rested after their long journey, perched on the slender towers of the Egyptian palace. Inside the palace, however, the mood was grim. The great and powerful ruler lay stiff as a mummy in the elaborately painted hall. His relatives and servants surrounded him. He was not dead, but neither was he alive. The swamp blossom which could save his life (if it were found and picked by the one who loved him most dearly) would never arrive. His young, beautiful daughter would never return.

"She is dead and gone!" reported the two princesses who had made the journey with her. Then they invented a little story about what had happened. "She was killed by the arrow of a hunter," they said. "We buried her and took

revenge on the hunter." They wept as they told the story. But the father stork who had heard the whole thing and knew what really happened rattled his bill in outrage!

"I'm going to steal those feathered capes from the two wicked princesses!" said the father stork. "We don't want those girls returning to the swamp to do more harm. I'll take the capes back to Denmark and hide them in our nest until I can find a use for them."

But let us hear, as the stork did, what took place the previous year, after the great ruler first become ill. The wise and learned had gathered to discuss how he could be cured. "Love nourishes life! The greatest form of love nourishes the highest quality of life!" they had said. Then they spoke endlessly about the different kinds of love and about the differences and similarities between them. At last they agreed again. "Love nourishes life, life to our great ruler." And in that statement lay a greater truth than they themselves understood. They repeated it over and over and had written it down like a prescription. But how it was to produce a cure was another problem.

Finally, they had agreed that help must come by way of the princess who loved her father with all her heart and soul. In a dream, the princess learned that she must bring a lotus blossom from a deep swamp in Denmark (the first blossom touched her breast beneath the water) if her father's life was to be saved. That is why she then flew in a feathered cape to the north. The swamp king had taken her down in the muddy swamp, and now her family believed she was dead. Only the very wisest of the wise admitted that no one knew for sure, so they would wait and see.

13

Back at the Viking log house in Denmark, the
baby girl was given the name Helga. It was a
name too sweet for a girl with such a temper.
The years passed quickly as she grew outwardly

14

more beautiful everyday, but inwardly more brutal and wild than most people of that dark age. The girl's stepmother was, by the standards and customs of her culture, a strong-willed and high-spirited woman. But towards Helga, she was soft and worrisome. What's more, it seemed as if the girl derived an evil enjoyment from discovering new ways in which to shock and frighten her stepmother.

There was but one thing which could tame Helga: twilight. As the sun began to go down each day, she became quiet and thoughtful, obedient and helpful. She was drawn by an inner compulsion to her stepmother's side. When the sun disappeared and the transformation was complete, she would sit silently in a corner with a melancholic expression on her ugly, frog-like face. Sometimes she would give a hollow croak like the softened sob of a child after a long cry. Then the Viking woman would take her up on her lap, forgetting the ugly appearance, look into her sad eyes and say, "I almost wish you could always be my silent frog-child. For you are more difficult to love when your beauty is turned inside out."

Early in the autumn of Helga's sixteenth year, the Vikings returned home with both plunder and prisoners. Among the prisoners was a young Christian priest, one of those who opposed worship of the Scandinavian heathen gods. This new faith, which had spread so widely in the south, was often discussed among the Viking warriors and their women. Even Helga had heard about Christ who willingly died out of love for mankind. But the stories went in one ear and out the other. The word "love" held no meaning for her. Her stepmother, however, listened and felt strangely moved by this talk about the Son of the only true God.

The young Christian prisoner was tied up and carried into the deep, stone cellar below the log house. He was to be sacrificed to the gods because he had denied and offended them. Helga asked for the privilege of sprinkling his blood on the paintings of the gods.

Later that evening, Helga's stepmother spoke to the ugly frog with passionate words of sorrow that poured from a broken heart. "Never have I dared to admit how miserably I suffer because of you. Great is a mother's love, but not once has this love penetrated your soul. Your heart is like a cold, muddy swamp! How did you ever come to my house?" she cried. She closed herself in behind the curtain which separated her bed from the rest of the room.

The frog was left alone in a corner. Big tears came to her eyes as she gave an occasional half-muffled cry of pain. It was as if she was labouring to give birth within the depths of her heart. Then she took a single step, listened, took another, then another and eventually lifted the heavy iron bar that locked the cellar door. Taking a burning torch with her, she silently descended the stone steps. In the damp cellar she woke the prisoner with her cold hand. She cut

16

the ropes that bound him and motioned for him to follow her.

At first the startled priest thought the hideous creature was an evil spirit. Yet he realized that she was filled with mercy. He followed her to a horse outside, and together they mounted and rode away. Before long they were out on the heath, far from the Vikings' house. As they rode along, the priest prayed and sang. The creature in front of him began to tremble. Was it caused by the power of prayer and praise, or by it the approaching dawn? She tried to jump from the horse, but the priest hung on and sang even louder. The horse continued to run, and the horizon turned red. As the first ray of sun broke through the clouds, the creature began to change.

17

At daybreak, the priest found himself with a beautiful young woman in his arms. Bewildered, he sprang from the horse. Helga followed and attacked him with a knife. She cursed him as she fought, but an unseen power lent its strength to the priest. At last Helga's feet became entangled in the roots of a tree, and she fell beside a tiny, bubbling spring. The priest sprinkled the fresh, cool water upon her and blessed her in the name of Christ, but the water of baptism has no power when faith does not bubble up from within as well. Still, a power greater than the strength of man prevailed over her. To Helga the Scriptures which the priest quoted and the prayers which fell from his lips seemed like a secret form of enchantment. Fascinated by it, she sank willingly into his arms like a tamed bird.

The priest spoke gently to Helga about the deed of love she had done towards him by setting him free. He said that the bonds which bound her were even stronger, but that she, too, could be set free and come to the light; she, too, could inherit eternal life. He tied two small branches together in the form of a cross and said, "The light from above has visited us, to shine on those who sit in darkness and to guide our feet on the path of peace."

Together the priest and Helga mounted the horse and rode into the forest towards the Christian city of Hedeby. The fresh air and the fragrance of the trees had a calming effect upon Helga, as did the gentle words of the priest. His heart was full of faith and Christian love, and he had an earnest desire to lead the young woman to God.

Just as drops of rain will hollow the hardest stone, the dew of God's grace began to soften the sharp edges of Helga's soul. Just as a mother's song will unconsciously be imprinted upon the heart of her child, so it was with the word of God and its creative power within Helga.

Helga and the young priest rode deeper into the forest. Towards evening they met a band of robbers. "Where have you found that beautiful girl?" shouted the robbers. One of them grabbed the horse and began to swing an axe. As the sun set, the priest and the horse lay dying of bloody head wounds, and the robbers took hold of Helga. At that moment she changed. Her pink lips became the wide, green mouth of the frog. Her slender white arms became slimy, webbed limbs. In fright, the robbers released her and scrambled away. Helga disappeared into the thicket with a sudden leap.

A full moon rose that evening. In its light the frog crept back to the bodies of the

Christian priest and the horse. She looked upon them with eyes that seemed to weep. She threw herself upon the one and then the other. Dead they were and dead they would remain. All night long she painstakingly worked to cover their bodies with leaves, branches, stones and moss.

At daybreak the girl Helga stood by their graves with bleeding fingers. For the first time ever tears rolled down her soft cheeks. The two natures battled within her. She trembled as if awakening from a frightful dream. All that day she stayed in the silent forest, attempting to endure the struggle in her heart.

Nightfall came at last, and Helga became the quiet frog. This time, however, there was a glint of humanity in her eyes that never before had shone, even as the beautiful maiden. This time her eyes were gentle, giving witness to something deeper. Those gentle eyes began to cry tears that came from her heart. She lifted the cross of branches which the priest had made, and planted it upon his grave. Then she scratched the shape of a cross into the earth. As she did so, the thick folds of skin fell from her hands like heavy gloves. Her lips began to quiver. She stammered as she spoke, "Jesus is the Christ." At these words, her frog shape fell away, and she was transformed into the young beauty again.

Now the murdered priest appeared to her, veiled by flames of light. She looked into his serious, kind eyes. They seemed to illuminate every crevice, every wrinkle of her heart. They illuminated her entire past. Each kind deed which had been done for her sake, and each loving word spoken to her came to memory. With these memories came the realization that a persistent love had sustained her through many difficult years. She, the offspring of soul and swamp, had followed only the voices of her own feelings, and had never helped herself at all. Yet, she had been given everything; and everything had been part of a greater plan. Bending her head in shame, she sensed a purifying flame go through her. It was the fire of the Holy Spirit.

"Daughter of the swamp," said the priest. "To those on earth, things seem to take a long time. Yet in eternity there is no such thing as time. One day you, too, will enter this eternal realm; but first you must fulfill the purpose of your life. Return to the place of your origin, break the shield of water, and pull up the living root from which you grew."

The priest lifted Helga upon the horse and mounted in front of her. Lifting the cross from the grave high into the air, they flew away. The cross shone like gold in the moonlight, and the open wound in the priest's head glittered like a diamond.

At last the horse and its riders circled the swamp by the Viking house. Helga and the priest sang a hymn as they passed over the muddy waters. At once the reeds began to blossom and green stalks began to shoot up. Before long the swamp was covered with water lilies. It looked like a colorful needlepoint blanket. Upon it lay a youthful-looking woman. Helga thought it was a reflection of herself in the water; but it was her mother, the Egyptian princess, wife of the swamp king. The woman was carried ashore by the horse, together with Helga. Then the horse and the priest dissolved into a fog that was blown away by the wind.

Mother and daughter stood beside the swamp and embraced each other, heart to heart. The mother's heart beat more rapturously, for she understood what had happened and who this beautiful maiden was. "My child, the blossom of my heart. My lily of the deep waters!" Her tears were a baptism of love for Helga.

The Egyptian princess told her own story to her daughter. As she did, the father stork flew above them and hurried back to his nest. He fetched the two feathered capes he had hidden so many years before and threw one down to each of the women. Then they rose from the earth as white swans.

"The water lily I was supposed to bring home is flying at my side!" said the princess. "Homeward! Homeward!" But Helga could not leave Denmark before she had once again seen her stepmother, the kind Viking woman. Helga felt, at last, a warm, compassionate love for her.

The two swans flew to the log house. Inside, everyone was peacefully asleep except the Viking woman. She lay half-awake, worrying about Helga, who had disappeared three days earlier with the Christian priest. The woman pondered the stories she had heard of the miracles of Christ and of those who believed in Him. These anxious thoughts became real in her dreams.

She dreamed she was still lying awake on her
bed, while outside it was dark and stormy. She
could hear the roar of the oceans. The spasms
and convulsions of giant sea monsters shook the
entire earth. It was the final hour for the heathen
gods. It was the end of the world. The horns
blew as the gods, clad in shining armour, rode
over the rainbow to fight the final battle. The
glare of the northern lights lit up the heavens, but
darkness was still victorious. It was a terrible
moment.

26

In her dreams the Viking woman reached down and lifted the ugly frog onto her lap. The frog shivered and cuddled up as her stepmother held her close and protectively. The air was pierced by the sound of rushing arrows and the clashing of swords. It seemed that heaven and earth would explode, and the stars would fall. Then the woman saw the gentle God of love released from the kingdom of the dead. She recognized His face. It was that of the imprisoned Christian priest.

"Jesus Christ!" she cried out. Then she kissed the frog-child in sheer joy. At that moment the frog shape fell away, and Helga sat beside her stepmother as beautiful as ever but sweet as never before. Helga kissed her, blessed her for the care she had given her, and thanked her for the loving thoughts she had sown and nurtured in her soul. Then Helga rose as a magnificent white swan and flew away with a mighty swoosh.

The Viking woman awoke to the sound of beating wings. She assumed it was the annual migration of storks over the house, and went to the door to say good-bye. Storks were everywhere: on the roof, in the trees, around the garden. But just opposite her, on the edge of the well, sat two swans. They looked at her with all-knowing eyes.

The woman remembered her dream and how she had seen Helga fly away as a swan. There was a mysterious sense of joy in her heart. She spread her arms out towards the two swans as she smiled through tears and a multitude of thoughts. The swans craned their necks in greeting and took to the air.

27

Back in the sunbaked land of Egypt lay the pale, withered ruler on his leopard-skin couch. He was neither dead nor alive. Suddenly, two white swans flew in through the palace window. They had arrived with the storks. The swans cast off their feathered capes and stood as beautiful women with long, hair, as blond and alike as two dewdrops. Helga bent over the body of her grandfather. As she did, the color returned to his cheeks, the light returned to his eyes, and life returned to his stiffened limbs. He rose up as if awakening from a long, heavy dream.

The gloomy atmosphere in the palace became one of great joy. While the Egyptian wise men quickly recorded the story of the princess and the healing blossom for the edification of the entire country, the storks told it in their own way to their children and later to their children's children.

That night when peace rested over the happy household, only one person remained awake. Helga stood on her balcony and looked out

28

through the clear sky at the twinkling stars. They seemed larger and brighter than in the north, and yet they were the same stars. They reminded her of her stepmother's eyes, and of the tears the woman had shed over her. They made her think of the glittering wound in the forehead of the young priest on the night they rode over the swamp. They brought to memory the shining words he had spoken about the great source of love which embraces all generations.

One autumn, a royal Arabian prince arrived at the Egyptian palace. He was as handsome as a prince should be! The palace had been proudly decorated for a wedding, and Helga was to be the bride. But at the wedding feast, Helga did not notice the tanned, manly face of her bridegroom, nor did she look into his fiery, dark eyes which fastened her in their gaze. She looked instead out towards the twinkling stars.

Suddenly the sky was filled with the rustle of stork wings. Helga rose from her place and went outside to greet them. Looking up, she saw the Christian priest approaching. He wanted to bless her on her wedding day. "But the radiance and glory of the kingdom of heaven outshines anything on earth!" he said.

Helga pleaded with him, begged him, to be able to peek into paradise for only a moment and see the Lord. So the priest lifted her up. It was as if a stream of melody and inspiration flowed around her and through her as well. Words could never describe it.

"We must return now; they'll miss you," said the priest.

"Only one last look, please . . ." Helga pleaded.

"We must return; the guests are leaving."

"Only one look, the very last . . ." And then Helga found herself outside the palace again. The lights had all been put out. The banquet hall was empty. Frightened, Helga ran through the corridors and bedchambers. Foreign soldiers were lying asleep there. She opened the door to her own room and stepped into a garden which had never been there before.

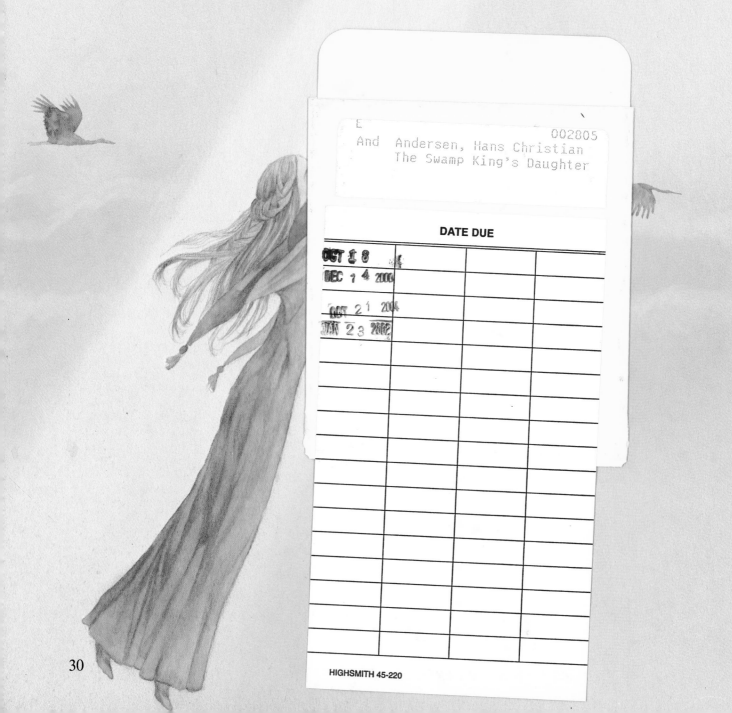